Pip & Squeak

Ian Schoenherr

SCHOLASTIC INC.
New York Toronto London Auckland
Sydney Mexico City New Delhi Hong Kong

Squeak pinched Pip,
and Pip squeaked.
"We're late," said Squeak.
"Don't forget the gift for Gus."

"Snow!" said Squeak.
"Get the sled!"

"Step on it, Pip!"

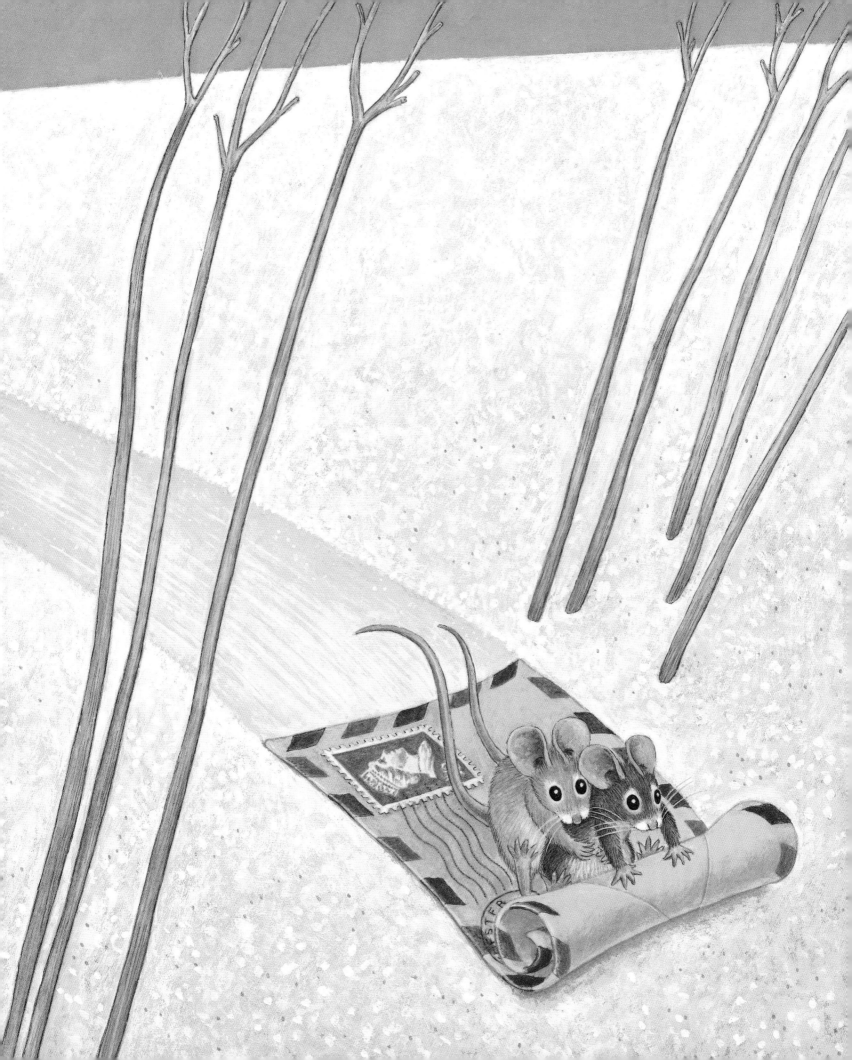

"Lickety-split!"

But then Squeak squinted at Pip . . .

"You forgot the cheese!" she said.
"Now what will we give Gus?"

"Something better?" Pip whispered,
and he slunk off to find it.

"This is great for Gus!" said Pip.

"Not as great as cheese," scoffed Squeak.

"Gus will love *this!*" said Pip.

"Is it full of cheese?" Squeak snorted.

Just then Pip saw something.
It was orange.

It was big.

"It's cheese!"

"Pip!"

squeaked Squeak.

Squeak scrambled down and pulled Pip up.

"It's not cheese, after all," sniffed Pip.

"We can still give it to Gus," said Squeak.

"He probably won't like it," said Pip.

But Gus thought it was perfect.

These mice are for my mother

ISBN 978-0-545-28803-3

12 11 10 9 8 7 6 5 4 3 2 1   10 11 12 13 14 15/0

Printed in the U.S.A.   08

This edition first printing, September 2010

Permanent ink and acrylic paint on watercolor paper were used to prepare the full-color art.
The text type is Hank.

These mice are for my mother

ISBN 978-0-545-28803-3

Copyright © 2007 by Ian Schoenherr. All rights reserved.
Published by Scholastic Inc., 557 Broadway, New York, NY 10012, by arrangement with Greenwillow Books,
an imprint of HarperCollins Publishers. SCHOLASTIC and associated logos are trademarks and/or
registered trademarks of Scholastic Inc.

12 11 10 9 8 7 6 5 4 3 2 1   10 11 12 13 14 15/0

Printed in the U.S.A.   08

This edition first printing, September 2010

Permanent ink and acrylic paint on watercolor paper were used to prepare the full-color art.
The text type is Hank.

But Gus thought it was perfect.